SUPERMAN
IS
COOPERATIVE

Written by
CHRISTOPHER HARBO

Illustrated by
GREGG SCHIGIEL

SUPERMAN created by
Jerry Siegel and Joe Shuster
by special arrangement with the
Jerry Siegel Family

PICTURE WINDOW BOOKS
a capstone imprint

Superman is cooperative. He always pitches in, and he works well with others. People know he will help them make the world a better place.

When Superman joins a team, he finds a way to help.

Superman cooperates by sharing the work.

When someone asks for help, Superman always lends a hand.

Superman cooperates by working together
to get the job done.

When Superman disagrees with someone's plan, he looks for the middle ground.

Superman cooperates by reaching a compromise.

When Superman works with others, he welcomes their strengths.

Superman cooperates by encouraging teamwork.

When Superman needs a hand,
he gladly accepts one.

Superman cooperates by allowing others to help him.

When Superman tackles a problem,
he asks for advice.

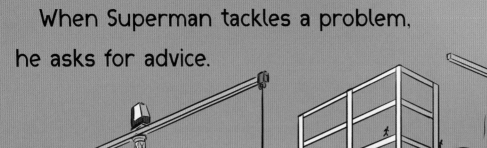

Superman cooperates by listening
to other peoples' ideas.

When Superman leads a team, he takes turns being in charge.

Superman cooperates by letting others serve as leaders too.

When something goes wrong, Superman admits his mistake.

Superman cooperates by always telling the truth.

Whenever evildoers are up to no good,
Superman steps forth to stop them.

And he never lets up until they cooperate!

SUPERMAN SAYS...

- Being cooperative means listening to others, like when I ask the construction workers for ideas before helping them fix the building.

- Being cooperative means helping others, like when I help Supergirl bring the plane in for a safe landing.

- Being cooperative means finding compromises, like when I help Lois Lane and Jimmy Olsen find a safe place to gather the news.

- Being cooperative means telling the truth, like when I tell the police officers it is my fault Lobo crushed their squad car.

- Being cooperative means being the very best you that you can be!

GLOSSARY

admit (ad-MIT)—to agree that something is true

advice (ad-VICE)—suggestions about what to do about a problem

compromise (KOM-pruh-mize)—an agreement that is reached when both sides in a disagreement give up some of their demands

disagree (diss-uh-GREE)—to have a different opinion

encourage (in-KUHR-ij)—to give praise and support

leader (LEE-duhr)—someone who leads a group of people

READ MORE

Cavell-Clarke, Steffi. *Helping Others.* Our Values. New York: Crabtree Publishing Company, 2018.

Harbo, Christopher. *Superman Is a Good Citizen.* DC Super Heroes Character Education. North Mankato, Minn.: Capstone Press, 2018.

Steinkraus, Kyla. *Let's Work Together.* Little World Social Skills. Vero Beach, F.L.: Rourke Educational Media, 2013.

INTERNET SITES

FactHound offers a safe, fun way to find Internet sites related to this book. All of the sites on FactHound have been researched by our staff.

Here's all you do:

Visit *www.facthound.com*

Type in this code: 9781515840206

23

DC Super Heroes Character Education
is published by Picture Window Books
A Capstone Imprint
1710 Roe Crest Drive
North Mankato, Minnesota 56003
www.mycapstone.com

Editor: Julie Gassman
Designer: Charmaine Whitman
Art Director: Hilary Wacholz
Colorist: Rex Lokus

STAR41228

Cataloging-in-Publication Data is available at the Library of Congress website.

ISBN: 978-1-5158-4020-6 (library binding)
ISBN: 978-1-5158-4287-3 (paperback)
ISBN: 978-1-5158-4024-4 (eBook PDF)

Printed and bound in India.
002620